Charles Newton-Robinson

Tintinnabula

New poems

Charles Newton-Robinson

Tintinnabula
New poems

ISBN/EAN: 9783744722797

Printed in Europe, USA, Canada, Australia, Japan

Cover: Foto ©Andreas Hilbeck / pixelio.de

More available books at **www.hansebooks.com**

TINTINNABULA

NEW POEMS

BY

CHARLES NEWTON-ROBINSON

BARRISTER-AT-LAW

LONDON

KEGAN PAUL, TRENCH, TRÜBNER & CO., LTD.

MDCCCXC

CONTENTS.

A BALLAD OF THE BATTLE OF CRÉCY.

PART I.

I know not whose the wrong was,
    And I know not whose the right
But well I wis at Crécy
    Was fought a gallant fight !

Short summons gave King Edward,
    Short summons wanted we ;
But more than thirty thousand men
    We crossed the Narrow Sea,
And very cold our welcome was
    In sunny Normandy !

We burnt Barfleur and Cherbourg,
    The cities of the coast ;
And like a whirlwind raging on,
We wrecked St. Lo, we ravaged Caen,

And if we did not sack Rouen
  The burghers cannot boast ;
For we saw their frighted faces
  Behind the bulwarks plain ;
But the only bridge was broken
  That spanned the surging Seine ;
And we were bound for Paris,
  So gave the leaguer o'er,
And onward pressed to rap our best
  Upon King Philip's door,—
To fire St. Germain, fire St. Cloud
  His very eyes before !

But when the sun of August
  Had turned the corn to gold,
And we used our swords for reaphooks,
  The Frenchmen grew more bold ;
For bitterly they grudged us
  The eating of their bread,
And weak to fight they judged us,
  With many sick or dead,

And many home at harvest,
  And not a few at sea,
Till out of thrice ten thousand,
  We were but one in three;
While round the oriflamme of France
  There flocked from every hand,
Beneath the banners of their lords,
  The legions of the land.

Hard rode the scouts the news to bring,
They saw Bohemia's blind old king
  Keep state in Philip's camp!
D'Alençon's count, and he of Blois,
  And John of rich Hainault;
  While not three marches off made halt
The hireling lances of Savoy,
  All men of sturdy stamp;
And more redoubted yet than these,
Full twice our force of Genoese,
  Who drew the steel crossbow:
  For not till after did we know

That all their engines, all their craft
Could never match the clothyard shaft
  Old England's yew can throw !

But only fools give battle
  Cooped up as in a pen,
Deep in a hostile country,
  When odds are one to ten ;
So day and night, and night and day,
We pressed upon our seaward way,
To snatch from Godemar du Fay
  The passage of the Somme ;
For such a hot pursuit was kept,
Eight nights together scarce we slept,
  So close the French had come ;
And gained we not the river
  To fend us from the foes,
Slight hope was to deliver
  Our bodies from the crows !

Late marched we on the morrow
  Till falling of the dew,

And halted at the hamlet
  Of Crécy, in Ponthieu.
Then a bold word spake King Edward :
  "Here let us take our stand !
Here will I wait mine enemy
  Upon my mother's land ;
For to my mother Crécy
  Belongs of marriage right,
And here let Philip Valois
  Make good his claim in fight !"

Then into three battalions
  The host he parted out,
The first and foremost of them
  The Prince of Wales about ;
And with the prince were chosen,
  The onset to abide,
The flower of England's chivalry,
  Her bulwark and her pride.

Marshal of all rode Warwick's earl,
  Next Oxford's courage rare,

With Kentish Cobham's warrior-lord,
  Bourchier and Delaware ;
While ever to be near the Prince
  Had fiery Chandos care.
Neville and Clifford, peers of fame,
With Latimer, not backward, came;
And knightly Harcourt's honoured name
  Rang through the morning air
From lip to lip ; nor be forgot
Mauley's and Stafford's temper hot,
  And Holland's eye of flame !

Yet none the less the French array
Kept gathering, from the break of day
  Until the heat of noon ;
And round us, where we stood at bay,
The space of half a mile away,
  Closed in a great half-moon.

As when the Netherlander,
  Behind his bulwark frail,

Sees bear on him the billows
  Blown skyward by the gale,
And fears the marshland acres,
  Which from the waves he won,
Four fathom deep will founder
  Before the tide has done ;
And trembles for his homestead,
  And trembles for his life ;
But like a man builds up the breach
  For home and child and wife :—
So we behind our breastwork
  Made head to that great host ;
Though not a soul among us all
But deemed himself or dead or thrall,
  —The fight already lost ;
Till forward came King Edward
  And rode from rank to rank ;
(A milk-white wand was in his hand,)
  His look so free and frank,
That but to gaze upon him
  Roused every fainting heart,

As graciously he smiled, and prayed
  Each man to do his part,
For God, for England, and the right
  And glory of his king,
And all the honour such a fight
  To every man must bring; '
For be it won, or be it lost,
To such an overwhelming host,
  Full wide the fame would ring !

PART II.

The space of half a mile away
Was halted still the French array;
Bright glinted in the clear noon-day
Their lances' points, their pennons gay;
And helm and corslet, sword and shield
Flashed lightly as the horses wheeled,
And plunged and tramped upon the ground,
With dull, confused, and threat'ning sound.

Now forth four knights came pricking,
  Their port was proud and high
Within an arrow-flight they came,
  Our order to espy.
The foremost rode the Lord le Moyne
  (We knew him by the shield
Which, after, with his life he left
  Upon the stricken field).
The names I mind not of the rest,
Though each proud helm bore figured crest,
And each, before he rode away,
Scanned every link of our array.

One only turned to jeer and laugh,
  Because we seemed so few,
And glancing back with scornful look,
Tall in his stirrup rose, and shook
  His gauntlet ;—then we knew
King Philip soon would try the right
  And title to Ponthieu.

And surely, ere an hour had sped
   The Frenchmen swarmed in front and flanks;
But like some rabble loosely led,
Soon as they met us face to face,
Their vanguard started back apace
   At sight of our close-ordered ranks,
Each man in his appointed place.

Backward and forward as they swung
   Through all King Philip came ;
A short while bent he on us
   A dark eye, lit with flame ;
The red blood rose in his sallow cheek,
   Black hate was at his heart ;
Then even to our farthest rear
   His harsh voice made men start :
" In God's name, and Saint Denis,
   I will that we engage !
Now forward with my Genoese,
   And let them earn their wage !"

Slow drew the bowmen to the fore
   As much against their will,
And while their tired and wavering ranks
   As yet were ordered ill,
Great marvels in the sky appeared:
   A cloud,—no common cloud!—
That high its billowy crest upreared,
   Swept over, thundering loud.
Between the armies aimed its track,
And all the sky behind was black.
And fluttering, screaming, on before,
   Like angry scolds at blows,
The whole sky o'er did wheel and soar
   A countless host of crows.
Yet not to right nor left they drew,
But straight between the foul birds flew!

And in their wake the air did shake,
   The lightning flashes quiver;
Like great sea-waves the thunder brake,
   The cloud did whirl and sliver;

And of this marvel, under breath,
  The wise among us said
It was a sign of battle dour,
  Where blood should freely shed !

Now when at last the Genoese
  Took heart with us to close,
From van to rear the word rang clear,
  " Advance ! and spring your bows ! "
Forward they came, ten steps or more,
  Fell sight it was to see !
Then with a shout the air they tore,
  But not a limb stirred we ;
Though twice again with might and main
  They shouted awesomely ;
And on the third cry sharp and loud,
  Their bolts came at us like a cloud !

But rain had sapped their bow-strings
  And marching made them tired,
And right before their faces
  The sunset flamed and fired ;

So many a bolt at random flew,
  And many a bolt fell short,
And truly, after such ado,
  Such little harm made sport !

But when these foreigners had felt
  The limit of their tether,
Up rose our English archers,
  All silent, all together,
And each man took one step in front,
  And each to ear drew feather :
My God !—the arrows from their bows
Flew thick and white as fly the snows,
  In wild and wintry weather !

What screams of pain and horror !
  What crowding in affright !
When on the foreign bowmen fell
  That fearful arrow-flight ;
While hot-head Frenchmen strove to hack
Through all the press a bloody track

To pierce to our assault;
And still amid the densest rout,
Our archers shot their quivers out,
Where no aim was at fault.

PART III.

Now thanks be to the archers
　The fight was well begun,
On the famous field of Crécy,
　At setting of the sun;
And thanks be to the archers
　The twilight fell before
The onset of the mounted knights
　And men-at-arms we bore;
When fierce D'Alençon smote us,
　With Flanders, good at pinch,

And all their vassal lances ;
   Yet could not make us flinch ;
For we around the Prince of Wales
   Gave backward not an inch ;
But thrust for thrust, and blow for blow
   We rendered back again ;
And hard, I trow, it was to know
   Who slew, and who were slain.

On stout d'Alençon's helmet
   Did Chandos ring his knell ;
The valiant Count of Flanders
   To earth did Cobham fell ;
Yet wilder grew the melée,
   And sorely we were pressed ;
The stout Savoyards gave us
   Nor breathing time nor rest.
They came on by the thousand,
   As billows of the sea ;
But like his rock-girt island
   Around the Prince stood we !

Keen on the watch, Northampton's earl
  Scented our parlous plight ;
No whit too soon he cried to aid.
  Ah ! 'twas a gladding sight
To see his fresh battalion,
  With many a lord and knight,
And nigh two thousand yeomen,
  All chafing for the fight,
Come striding in their order
  Full cheerly, with a cheer,
Through to the battle's border
  Quick pressing from the rear !
Down dropped the German foemen
  As trees before the blast ;
Like sheep ran Genoa's bowmen ;
  Savoy fell back at last !

" Thanks, brave Northampton, thanks ! "
  Warwick cried :
" Noble peers, gallant knights,
Close your ranks ! close your ranks !

Bear the wounded to the rear!
Bide the foe; have no fear
But he'll charge us once again,
 And the turning of the tide
  Is not yet!
Look! the lancers of Lorraine
Are thick upon the plain!
Man to man, spear to spear,
  Be they met!

" But thou, Sir Thomas Norwich,
 Spur to the King and say,
' Sire, on the word of Warwick!
 The field is yours to-day,
If but your own battalion
 May join us in the van!
Now forward with the standard,
 And forward every man!

"' The Prince, and we about him,
 Who bear the battle's brunt,

Are hard beset—our wounds are wet,
  Our blades are waxing blunt ;
Our arms grow weak, and we are few ;
  'We stand, and do not blench,
But scarce may we avail to rout
  The remnant of the French.' "

The good knight pricked his charger's flank,
  Flew bounding up the hill,
And sharp drew rein before the King,
  Hard by the very mill
That still is on the windy top,
  From whence he might descry
The changing fortune of the field,
  Plain underneath his eye.

But when Earl Warwick's charge was told,
  Sternly King Edward said :
" My son is he but overborne ?
  Or is he stark and dead ?
Or hath he such a grievous wound,
  That all his strength is sped ?"

" Not so, Sir King ! " the knight returned,
  " But rudely set upon !
And may the Prince but have your aid,
  He counts the battle won ! "

" Back ! " quoth the King, " Back ! back again !
  To those from whom you hied,
And straitly charge my son and them,
  That whatsoe'er betide,
So long as breath is in his lips,
  They ask no aid of me !
Let the boy win his spurs, I say !
  For an God's will it be,
Mine is, the day shall be his own,
The honour his and theirs alone ! "

Now not a man but when he heard
Drew courage from King Edward's word.
And, glory be to God on high !
  Great deeds of arms were wroken,
The stout Lorrainers, forced to fly,
  Like wasted waves were broken.

By Heaven ! English hearts are true,
And reck not, though they be but few ; '
And English arms are stout and strong !
Fierce was the battle, though not long,
And ours the mast'ry; yet amid
All feats of arms the darkness hid,
Bohemia still may vaunt with pride
Her ancient king's last knightly ride !

His charger in the forefront paced
   Soon as the fight grew hot ;
A grey beard from his gorget flowed,
   Visor his helm had not ;
But three white ostrich feathers
   Were waving in his crest,
And large of mould, though few and old,
   His knights around him pressed.

Bolt upright in the saddle sat
   The man of eighty winters ;
He heard the wave of battle break,
The hissing noise the arrows make,

The stifled moan of man and horse,

The heavy fall of corse on corse,

When axe and sword on armour crashed

And horse and man to earth were dashed,

   And lances flew to splinters ;

And he spake to the Lord le Moyne, say
     they,

   Who live to tell the tale—

(Never a trustier knight had he

   Than the lord of towered Basèle,)—

And the words of the King were, " How goeth
     the fight ? "

   And the truth he heard from his trusty
     knight.

" Ha ! " said the King, " ill doth it ring !

   How fareth Charles, my son, this day ? "

One answered him, " We know not, sire !

   But think he joineth in the fray."

For the bitter truth none wished revealed,

That the craven already had left the field.

The King reined in his charger ;
   "Brothers in arms !" cried he,
" All friends of mine and lieges,
   Brave gentlemen, are ye !
And since these eyes are sightless,
   Give aid unto your lord,
And lead me far enough to strike
   One good stroke of my sword !"

They looked at one another,
   All silent for dismay ;
They knew that death was certain,
   Yet would not disobey ;
They tied their reins together,
   His vassals old and grey ;
And so they led their old blind king
   Right forward in the fray.

They fell upon our archers,
   And broke them through and through ;
They fell upon our foremost ranks,
   Like valiant men and true ;

But round them closed the archers,
   And set on them again,
And in the darkness of the night
   Down dropped they with the slain !

CECILY.

If at the sudden sight of thee
  Joy pulses through my brain,
It is not love ; but I foresee,
  —Fair rose, to bloom so fain !—
The peerless woman thou wilt be,
One day, my sweet girl Cecily !

I gaze beyond thy semblance now,
And in that wide-expanding brow,
With archèd eyes of soft blue-gray ;
—Like the tender dawn of day—
Trusting eyes, that dare be seen,
Telling pure thoughts—nothing mean;
And in thy bearing, firm and mild,
I see the woman through the child.

Like a perfect image, wrought
Only in the sculptor's thought;
Like a new song, under breath,
   A poet-lover sings;
Like a late-born butterfly,
   Sunning her moist wings;
Like a young moon lit anew;
Like a glad dream, coming true;
All delights too fresh to cloy!
Like all these art thou, my joy!

AMORIS IMAGO.

'Tis but in dreams that I have met my love,
    And where she walks I know not, on this earth ;
    Whose child she is, or what her day of birth ;
And yet what know I not, that love can move ?

Uncalled she came, at dead of morning night,
    In such apparel as might angels wear ;
    Brown-eyed as breaking dawn, with golden hair,
As gilds a cloud the first faint shoot of light.

I lay entranced, as though my lips were dumb,
    My brain, my sense for very joy adaze :.
    Awhile she bent on me her ardent gaze,
Then said, " You wished for me, and I am come ! "

THE BEE AND THE PRIMROSE.

Where bloomed a primrose in the north,
When the spring sun first came forth,
A wild bee wended from the south,
Humming song with honied mouth;
But ever as he northward flew,
Days were colder, flow'rets few;
Then his lays, begun so gladly,
Lost their theme, and ended sadly,
And his flight so straight and strong
Wandered idly, like his song.
At last upon a garden bed
For shelter till the snows were sped,
Weak and weary, and affrighted,
Down to gather strength he 'lighted;
But when once his wings relaxed,
Gross as leaden weights they waxed,
On his eyes a twilight fell,

And much he feared the cowslip's bell
Could only blow to ring his knell;
For the crocus, over-bold,
And the snowdrop, icy cold,
No honey-sweet for him could hold.

A child went through the garden gate.
Into the wood she stept, elate;
The firstling primrose there she found,
Sequestered in the coppice ground.
She lifted it, both root and head,
And in the warm and sheltered bed,
Where the wild bee sank as dead,
She planted like a garden flower,
The foster-child of sun and shower.
Then rising from her bended knee,
Chanced to espy the fainting bee,
And hardly thinking what she did,
Him among the petals hid,
—The primrose petals, pale and young
That peeped the tender leaves among.

LOVE'S MESSENGERS.

Wind, happy river, to the sea,
Whereby she dwells, who loves not me,
And waft her from this inner moat
The spoils that on thy waters float,
  My messengers to be !

Thrice happy river ! wind among
Spring-kissed arbours, green and young,
And waft my love all gentle things
That love has caught on giddy wings,
  And on thy mercy flung.

Aye, waft her all thou makest prize
Of birds and bees and butterflies,
And waft her branches new in bud
Thou reivest from thy banks in flood,
  When rain bedims the skies.

Wind, happy river ! to the sea,
And bear these messages for me !
But if no kind reply come back
Ere swallows take their southern track,
Myself thy spoil will be !

NOCTIS SUSURRUS.

Rest awhile, and hear me, sweet !
  Here are none to lurk and spy :
Close the branches round us meet,
  Vainly through the blackness pry
Myriad, myriad starry eyes !
We are sheltered from surprise ;
Owl and moth alone may see
What shall pass 'twixt thee and me !

It is dark, and yet not dark :
  Light is in those eyes of thine !
Still, so still the night is,—hark !
  I can hear thy heart and mine !
Kiss me, sweet ! and closer press !
Give me back my lips' caress !
If my timid tongue be still,
Think no ill, sweet ; think no ill !

Is it time? O is it time?
  Have I served thee long enough?
Will my venture seem a crime?
  Dare I ever risk rebuff?
No, I dare not, though I long;
Love itself has tied my tongue!
Lest I lose thee, love, for life,
I fear to whisper " Be my wife!"

Ah! but thou hast overheard!
  Else what means this tell-tale thrill?
Did I breathe a spoken word?
  Night so treacherously still!
Forgive me, sweet; forgive? forget!
If I am over-bold, but yet,—
Press closer, sweet!—when all is told,
Am I, am I,—over-bold?

THE CRUSADER'S HOME-COMING.

The Lady's orisons are low
  As is her conscience light ;
I hear no word,—but well I know,
  Her prayer is for her knight.

Between the branches of the vine
That round about her window twine,
He watches, in the cold moonshine,
Whom she believes in Palestine,
Bearing the blood-red cross right well
For Christ against the infidel.

And he, who never feared the Moor,
Comes trembling to his lady's door !
He trembles ; for the four long years,
  Since his departure sped,

Are fraught with hopes, and fraught with fears,
   For she may deem him dead ;
And men are bold and women frail,
And greed of gold might work him bale,
Since wide estates tempt even a friend,
To deeds which heart's blood will not mend.

The Lady's orisons are spoken ;
   But hark !—within !—a louder noise !
   And surely of another voice !—
Bolt and bar the knight has broken ! ·
   Like a whirlwind enters he !
   But only, glad in soul, to see
   His own child on its mother's knee,
Of constant love the token !

HARING OF HORN.

Spanish Don Frederic,
    Fiend out of hell !
Hemmed in proud Haarlem,
    Leaguered it well ;
None let he enter,
    Gentle or knave ;
None let he leave it,
    But for the grave !

Then wrote the burghers,
    —Wrote it in blood,
Pinned on a dove's wing—
    "Give us but food,
William of Orange !
    Staunch are we all ;
Yet if we starve, then
    Haarlem must fall ! "

Light though his treasure,
   Succour he sent ;
Few though his army,
   Freely they spent
Blood for their brothers,
   On the dyke side ;
One against seven ;
   Venged ere they died.

Such odds the stoutest
   Long cannot stay.
Woe unto Haarlem !
   Once they give way.
Ha ! they retreat now,
   Sore overpressed !
Many are butchered,
   On the dyke's crest.

" Who dares the hot foe
   Here to abide,
Where the dyke narrows,
   Midst of the tide?"

" That will I gladly,
  All hope forlorn ! "
Manfully answered
  Haring of Horn.

On came the Spaniards,
  Thirsting for blood ;
Well was the way barred !
  Backward they stood.
On came the Spaniards,
  Burning for shame ;
Little recked Haring
  How many came !

" Harder you push me,"
  Shouts he in scorn,
" Harder you'll find me, —
  —Haring of Horn ! "
Thus a full half hour,
  Stands he at bay,
Watching the rearmost
  Safely away.

Now from his fresh wounds
   Quick the blood flows;
" Ask and have quarter ! "
   Tempt him the foes.
Prouder his glance is,
   Louder his scorn:
" Only of God begs
   Haring of Horn ! "

" Still knows he one way
   Freedom to save ! "
Speaking, he plunges
   Into the wave !
Bolder no heart is,
   Truer no arm ;
God be his buckler,
   Shield him from harm !

AD UXOREM.

Sweet fellow-voyager with me
Through life's unlit, uncharted sea !
My gentle queen ! to whom I own
The fealty of love alone ;
Two golden years are gone to-day,
Since first I gloried in your sway,
And sealed my homage with a vow ;
—Years once of hope, of memory now ;
But happier far, in retrospect,
Than even sanguine Hope had recked,
Peering with her lovelit eyes
Through the future's darkling skies !

NYCTALOPÆ.

Blind go the many through the world ;
  Worm-battening moles, they delve unseen,
  Their dark and tortuous ways between
  The start and sordid goal of lives unclean :
And should there be uphurled,
In those chance gropings, any grass-tipt sod,
  And some emerge to feel the sunny ray,
    They own the warmth, and smile,
    And call it day ;
But the clear light, the gift of God,
    They cannot see, and having sunned awhile,
Again to that grave-dwelling-house descend,
Wherein their birth is, and wherein their end.

A ROMANCE OF THE STREETS.

I walk to Town by crowded ways
    Every morning early :
The sights I see, the sounds I hear,
Move pity, wonder, even fear ;
    But gladness,—rarely.

When at the crossing, day by day,
    I turn to Lincoln's Inn,
The same small sweeper begs of me,
    —A lad so pale and thin,
That much I doubt the sweeping trade
    Half starves the manikin.

A hard and sordid world it is,
    This of the London streets !
Yet, now and then, a sunny ray
    Across the darkness fleets.
The sweeper's days are not all sad ;
Even his world, by fits, is glad.

This very morning what saw I,
  In passing near his haunt ?
A tiny girl-mite, plump and round,
  Beside his figure gaunt ;
A ten-year-old, bright, foreign birdie,
Chirping to the hurdygurdy.

The pretty child had hazel eyes,
  Large lips that pout to kiss,
And soft Italian, sunburnt cheeks ;
  For not a month it is
Since for some fœtid London alley,
Her parents left their Lombard valley.

A gay bandanna neckerchief
  Was tied below her chin ;
A rude rough pair of sandal-shoes
  Her ten toes nestled in ;
Her shawl ! you seldom see its fellow
For startling hues,—her frock, bright yellow

She stood, half-scared, among the crowd
   That hasted careless by ;
The hurdygurdy's grating wheel
   Her baby hands made fly :
While notionless of tune or time,
The baby mouth sang seesaw rhyme.

I must have frowned, and shut my ears,
But that beforehand started tears ;
For at the quaint musician's side
My starveling sweeper stood tongue-tied,
Rapt, joyous, still, and wonder-eyed.

He watching her, she watching him,
   Between her tresses curly ;
He thought she played like Joachim,
She deemed him as the Anakim,
   —So big, and tall, and burly.

His very rags to her are dear,
Her clamour cannot shock his ear

For love can be as deaf as blind,
    And his makes music of her noise,
    And to her foes—big dogs and boys—
      Nerves him a champion dread ;
She, gratefully and shyly kind,
    Divides with him her bread.

A CRY OF THE STREETS.

"Buy a light ! buy a cigar light ! "
  Pitiful whine ! I hear it yet,
  And see her shivering, cold and wet,
In the star-light—in the star-light :
A woman's form, but an eldritch hag !
  When I turn, her face to see,
  White as a skull on a gallows tree,
With a bonnet-remnant of murky rag,
Like the felon's last lock of tangled hair,
Fluttering loose in the ice-cold air !

The chilly moon set early to-night,
And it wants eight hours to the dawning light.
Like a wicked spirit in ire or fright,
The north gale sweeps the empty street
With fitful showers of biting sleet,
It has blown the flaring gas-lights out,
And driven the starving tramps to rout :

The only sound, as I homeward pace,
 One lone policeman's rigid tread,
The echoing length of Portland Place,
 Half-muffled on the pavement dead,
And the chimes that brokenly noise the hour
From many a near and far-off tower,
For London is fast asleep ;
And who that can help it would vigil keep?
And·now again all sounds are still,
But for some railway whistle, shrill,
Wafted miles by the stifled gale,
That chokes and would shriek, but can only wail !

Silent and black the houses frown,
Looking coldly and careless down
On the homeless wretch in the star-light :
And mixing with the windy woe,
Again I hear the whimper low,
 " Buy a light ! buy a cigar light ! "
While fearful of the beggars' law
 We lightly heed who live at ease,

She proffers, with hand like a sick bird's claw,
   One frowsy box of damp fusees :
"Buy a light ! buy a cigar light !"
      And O, the pity !
      Wealthy city !
There should be any like her to-night.

MERIDIEM VERSUS.

Steadily 'thwart the Channel tide
Her paddle-fins my steamer plied,
  And like a dazzling diadem
  Thickly sown with gem on gem,
Stars in daylight, flashed and shone,
—Sea-children of an April sun,—
  The ripples at her stem.
But I was bound for sunnier seas,
Beyond the frozen Pyrenees,
That kiss the shores of Spain ;
  Where Barcelona's haven wide
  Is gay with argosies that ride
A bluer, brighter main !

E

So on thy northern threshold, France,
I landed; not with shield and lance,
  As did our sires of eld;
But swallow-like, with curious zest,
To travel as a flitting guest
  Through heritages held
In thraldom once, by force and fear
Of Crécy, Agincourt, Poitier.

Then gliding on the iron track,
  (New link of conquering France with Spain,
  More close than old bonds forged in vain,)
With often a long look back,
Far, far too fast, I hurried past
  A wide town-studded plain;
A minster here, a fortress there,
To take it were a king's despair,
  Though oft, I warrant, girt with foes,
  It felt the worst of hunger's throes.
And once there came a glimpse so fair,
The thought has ever since made rise
Sweet tears in too-contented eyes:

A sunlit valley, far below
  My track (that on a mountain hung),
  Where a bright streamlet wound among
Green meadows mapped like spiders' webs,
  And fringed with poplar, elm, and oak,
Tiny as mosses underfoot ;
  With white-walled hamlets, breathing smoke,
So far below, they seemed but toys,
  At feet of mountain-children scattered :
So far below, life made no noise,
  No echoes on the peaks were shattered !
A heaven of dreams, a haven of rest,
To satisfy a poet's quest !

      *   *   *   *   *

An evening went, a morning came,
And burning with a clearer flame
  Than lights Thames' chilly ooze,
I saw the southern sun's red rim
Swift upward from the dark earth swim
  By half-awake Toulouse.

As one who seeks and cannot find,
Felt I how far was left behind,
   My verdant, misty home ;
For strange to me the Afric breeze,
And strange the gray-green olive trees,
   Bare vines, and barren loam ;
And yellow oxen, yoke on head,
Before the plough, with lurching tread,
   By swarthy peasants driven ;
And rocky rivers dried to rills,
And naked sands, and arid hills,
   Where blade has never thriven.

To sea ! to sea ! arrest not me,
   Sad realm of thirst and fire !
I will not stay, though Carcas[1] call
Down from her beetling, crag-set wall :
   " Turn, traveller with the lyre !
Greet me, for I am fair and tall,
   And need no foil of rich attire,

   [1] See note, p. 81.

I who am ever young !
Have not I heard sweet odes in many a tongue,
  Since the old founders of this fortress town
  Chose me for guardian of the civic crown,
And wilt thou pass me by, unhailed, unsung?"

" Farewell !" I answered; "mine are willing ears,
And eager eyes ; but full, too full, of fears
Thy beauty strange ! my love is not so bold
That I may dare a dalliance with thy charms,
To be enwithered in thy scorching arms,
Though ever young, immeasurably old !
Too many loves, too many lovers, thine !
  As many as the years that leave no trace
  On thy still, marble face.
What mortal life may link with life divine,
But soon it flickers out and fades away,
  As from thy battlements at set of sun
The unregarded glimmer of a day,
  That hath been fair, and yet its course hath
    run !

" Farewell !—farewell !—what far-off peaks are
  these ?

  What snowy peaks that scale the sky ?

The Pyrenees ! the Pyrenees !

Their feet are in the summer seas,

  And thither bound am I ! "

IN BURGOS CATHEDRAL.

This liquid eve how loth expires
The radiance of the sunset fires !
And still the deep'ning flood of blue
Forbears to quench their flaming hue,
From all the whilom golden West
By " heavenly alchemy" expressed.

In such a gloaming, once, in Spain,
By stately Burgos' minster fane,
I sat and watched the glory vanish
—As long it hath from all things Spanish—
And not before the evening star
Sailed upward in her silver car,
And chilly dews and bats were free,
Did I arise from reverie,

And steal to tread, by postern door,
The dim cathedral's echoing floor,
Through dusky aisles, where nothing stirs
But pious feet of worshippers,
Who slowly pass from grille to grille,
And thumb their beads, demure and still,
At every altar-sheltering arch
That waits them on their reverent march.

I mused an hour, as rapt as they,
Till dusk had sealed the eyes of day,
And evened with the gloom below
The western window's ruby glow.
Sudden out rang the vesper bell,
It rent the silence, broke the spell.
To touch the flying lamps with flame
The taper-lifting vergers came,
And eager to be purged of sin,
A vulgar, laughing throng pushed in ;
Father and mother, son and daughter,
Duly besprent with holy water.

Then oh ! what hubbub, noise and rustle,

Mundane chatter, coughs and bustle !

But half-abashed for anthem-singing,

Banner-waving, censer-swinging,

Torches flickering, gilt robes glancing,

Priests in solemn file advancing,

With choristers, canonicos

Parting left and right in rows,

—Canonicos obese and puffy,

Canonicos grim, gaunt, and huffy,

Niching each in carven stall ;

But stout or thin, and short or tall,

And whether worldly dogs or purists,

All self-complacent sinecurists !

ECHOES

OF

FRENCH POETRY.

THE BALLADE

WHICH VILLON WROTE, EXPECTING TO BE HANGED.

Ye brother men ! who after us live on,
Let not your hearts too hard against us grow ;
For if you pity us poor wights, anon
To you the rather God will mercy show.
Here you see us hung ; five—six—in a row !
As for the flesh that once we pampered gaily,
It is piecemeal devoured, and rotting daily
And we, the bones, to dust and ashes fall.
At our ill chance, O neither laugh nor rail ye,
But pray to God that he absolve us all !

If we cry on you, brothers, you must not
Mete us disdain ; though justice, for offence,
Put us to death ; since none the less you wot
That not all men have got enough good sense.
Then intercede for us, with prayer intense,
Before the sweet Son of the Virgin Mary,

That unto us His grace may never vary,
Which hindereth Hell-fire our souls to thrall.
Dead are we ; us then let no mortal harry,
But pray to God that he absolve us all !

The rain has washed and drenched us from the skies ;
The sun has dried us up, and burnt us brown ;
Magpies and crows have hollowed out our eyes,
And rooted forth the hairs of beard and crown.
Never one instant have we sat us down :
Now here, now there, howso the breezes vary,
Swung at their pleasure, we may never tarry ;
Pecked, thick as thimble-dents, by birds withal.
Mortals ! no mocking speeches hither carry,
But pray to God that he absolve us all !

ENVOI.

Prince Jesus ! who o'er all hast seignory,
Care Thou that Hell gain not the mastéry !
Us may no commercing with Hell befall !
Men ! be not ye of our fraternity ;
But pray to God that he absolve us all !

THE ROSE.

Sweet heart ! let us look if the rose,
In the morning so fain to disclose
Her purple attire to the sun,
Has not lost with the waning of day,
The folds of her crimson array,
And her blush, like yours alone !

Ah ! see in how short a space,
Sweet heart ! she has littered the place
With her beauty, alas ! in a shower !
O Nature ! hard stepmother, sure,
If such a fair bloom can endure
But from dawn to the vesper hour.

Then if you will trust in me, sweet !
So long as your life's budding yet,

In its radiance green and new,

Cull the blossom of youth when it blows

For as old age dealt with the rose,

It will wither your beauty too !

(RONSARD.)

BARCAROLLE.

O maiden fair and young,
  Say where would you be going?
The sail aloft is hung ;
  The breeze will soon be blowing !

My flag's of silken-gores,
Of ivory my oars,
  My rudder purest gold ;
An angel's wing's my sail,
My crew's a cherub hale,
  And an orange crams my hold !

O maiden fair and young,
  Say where would you be going?
The sail aloft is hung ;
  The breeze will soon be blowing !

Let's roam Pacific waves,
Or where the Baltic raves,
  Or far as Java's isle ;
Or else to Norway go,
To pluck the flower of snow,
  And time and care beguile !

O maiden fair and young,
  Say where would you be going ?
The sail aloft is hung ;
  The breeze will soon be blowing !

" O bring me," she replied,
" To that true river's side,
  Where love dwells evermore ! "
—Alas ! my darling maid,
In Loveland, I'm afraid,
  We never knew that shore !

                (TH. GAUTIER.)

FAREWELL.

Farewell ! I know that in this life
    I never may behold thee more.
God came ; forgot me, summoned thee ;
    And, losing thee, I learn what love I bore !

Not a tear ! not a barren sigh !
    The Future's due respect I pay.
And come the veil that bears thee off,
    With smiles will I behold it pass away.

Full of hope thou art taking leave ;
    In pride will thy home-coming be ;
But those who ever must thine absence mourn
    Shall wait unrecognized of thee.

Farewell ! thou wilt dream a fair dream,
    And be enfevered of a dread delight ;

Upon thy road, long yet, the rising star
　Will shed a dazzling glamour o'er thy sight.

Thou too, some day, perchance wilt learn
　The meed of one responsive heart ;
The good that's gained by knowing it,
　The misery to be torn apart !

　　　　　　　(A. DE MUSSET.)

A DECEMBER NIGHT.

Before my schoolboy days took flight,
I sat up reading, late one night,
The classroom's loneliness my plea :
   To sit with me, behind my back
   A poor child stole up, dressed in black ;—
No brother could be more like me.

His countenance was grave and fair ;
And by the candle's feeble glare
He came to read my open book,
   And leant his forehead on my palm ;
   Remaining till the morrow, calm
And pensive ; yet with smiling look.

My fifteenth year but just complete,
I trod one day with loitering feet,

Within a wood, a grassy lea.
  A stripling came, all clothed in black,
  And sat him down beside my track ;—
No brother could be more like me.

I prayed him tell which path were mine.
He bore a bunch of eglantine ;
On the other arm his lute lay still.
  Save greeting kind, he nought replied,
  But mutely, turning half aside,
With finger pointed up the hill.

What time I put my trust in love,
As closely to my room I clove,
Bewailing some first misery,
  There came to sit before my fire
  A stranger clothed in black attire ;—
No brother could be more like me.

His mien was dark, with troublous eyes ;
One hand he pointed at the skies,

The other flashed a dagger's gleam
　He seemed to suffer all my grief;
　Yet, snatching but a sigh's relief,
He vanished like an empty dream.

Then came the age when youth is wild.
To drink a harlot's health beguiled,
One night I raised my cup, to see
　A boon-companion take his place,
　In garb of black, before my face ; —
No brother could be more like me.

He wore beneath his mantle new
Some tattered rags of purple hue ;
His forehead budless myrtle crowned ;
　His wasted arm was held to mine,
　And, touching his, my cup of wine
This quaking hand let slip to ground.

Another year, as daylight fled,
I knelt before a dying bed ;

My father's—there again was he !
   Beside the deathbed of my sire
   An orphan crouched, in black attire ;—
No brother could be more like me.

His eyes were drowned in tears, like those
Of angels weeping human woes ;
His brows were decked with wreathèd thorn ;
   Upon the earth his lute was laid,
   Blood-hues his purple vest betrayed,
A dagger cleft his bosom lorn.

So well do I recall him yet,
His face I never shall forget
A moment, all my life's career.
   A vision very strange, I wis ;
   But whether fiend or angel 'tis,
The friendly shade seems everywhere.

When, later, overtaxed with pain,
To end it, or be born again,

I doomed myself exile from France;
　And when, impatient to be gone,
　I hurried forth, to seek alone
Some vestiges of Hope, perchance;

At Pisa, 'neath the Apennine;
Cologne, upon the banks of Rhine;
At Nice, along the valley-side;
　At Florence, in her palace halls;
　At Briguës, 'twixt the cottage walls,
Upon the drear Alp's bosom wide;

In Genoa's citron-shaded ease;
At Vevey, 'neath the apple-trees;
At Havre, by the Atlantic wave;
　At Venice, on the foul Lidò,
　Where Adria's pallid billows flow,
To swoon upon a grassy grave;

Wherever, 'neath the vasty skies,
I have tired my heart and eyes,

Bleeding from a cureless wound ;
　Wherever lame Ennui, in league
　With sullen, spiritless Fatigue,
Has drawn me on a harrow, bound ;

Wherever, raging ceaselessly
With thirst of worlds unknown to me,
The spectre of my dreams I chase ;
　Wherever, though I have not been,
　I see again,—too often seen !—
Through clouds of lies—the human face.

Wherever, too, along my road,
My brow upon my hands I load,
And like a woman, sob despair ;
　Wherever, like a lamb forlorn,
　That strews his fleece upon the thorn,
I feel my very soul grow bare ;

Wherever I would sleeping lie ;
Wherever I have longed to die ;

Ay, wheresoe'er on earth I flee ;

   There comes to sit beside my track

   A wretch attired in garb of black;

No brother could be more like me !

              (A. DE MUSSET.)

TO-MORROW.

None the future can control ;
The future God alone can tell.
Sire ! each time the hour doth toll,
All creation cries farewell !
Futurity,—'tis mystery !
All the things on earth that be,—
—Fame, and fortune soldierly :
Crowns that dazzle subject eyes :
Victory, with singèd wings :
Pride of glory-sated kings :—
Are only as the bird that springs
Lightly on the roof, and flies !

No, none ; though masterful, no man, by mirth or
　　tears,
Can force thy lips to speak, or, till the hour
　　appears,
　　Thy chilly grip forestall ;

O spectre mute ! O shadow ! O dread host !
O stealthy-following, ever-maskèd ghost,
    Whom men " To-Morrow " call !

        Oh ! To-Morrow laughs at laws !
        Ask you what to-morrow sends ?
        Man to-day will sow the cause,
        To-morrow God matures his ends.
        To-morrow !—lightning dulled in cloud,
        Fog that dims the starry crowd,
        And traitor yet but half-avowed !—
        'Tis the ram that breaks the wall ;
        'Tis a path-forsaking sun ;
        'Tis Paris aping Babylon !
        To-morrow is the frame of the throne,
        To-day is the velvet pall !

To-morrow—'tis the charger that falters, foamy
    white ;
To-morrow, conqueror!—'tis Moscow fired by night,
    As a torch lit in the gloom !

To-morrow your Old Guard strew, dead, for mile
    on mile,
The plain of Waterloo ;—then lone St. Helen's
    isle !
  And then, and then—the tomb !

    Great citadels to you unbar
    At summons of your charger's heel ;
    You cut the knot of civil war,
    By the keen edge of the steel ;
    You, my chief ! alone can chain
    The haughty Thames, in her disdain,
    And fickle Victory make fain
    To own your clarion hers !
    You can pass where keys are lost,
    Put to shame the proudest boast,
    And set for star before a host
    The rowel of your spurs !

God keeps Eternity, but still he leaves you Space ;
Yours is on earth the grandest, highest place
    Man ever had that under heaven trod !

Sire ! you can take at will, and at a bound,

Europe from Charlemagne and Asia from Mahound !

—But not the Morrow from the eternal God !

(VICTOR HUGO.)

NOTE.

Built into the wall of the very ancient hill city of Carcassonne, near the Narbonne gate, is a female head, rudely carved in grey stone, over which are inscribed the words

"SVM CARCAS."

This piece of sculpture is said by tradition to represent a Saracen lady called Carcas, not as her own proper name, but because she was reputed the lady and queen of Carcassonne. The story is that after the fortress had been five years invested by Charlemagne, had lost nearly all its defenders and was threatened by famine, this lady with many ingenious stratagems beguiled the emperor into raising the siege. But as soon as his forces began to move away, she ordered the bells to be rung, and throwing open the gates went forth to salute her great adversary, who, admiring her courage and resource, made her a present of the city she had so valiantly defended, and gave her in marriage to one of his peers.